# The Jump

Jessica DiPalma

NFB
Buffalo, New York

NFB
<<<>>>
NFB Publishing/Amelia Press
119 Dorchester Road
Buffalo, New York 14213

For more information visit Nfbpublishing.com

In Memory of C.C.

# Chapter One

As Jack Saunders was hurtling through the air above the lunch yard of his New York City Public School, he had time to think about the recent events in his life. It hadn't taken long for everything to go horribly wrong.

Things began to take a turn for the worse when his mother's boyfriend informed her that he had met someone new and was leaving. Then to make matters much worse she lost her job. His aunt had found his mom a new job, but it involved moving.

Through it all Jack had been promised things would get better; but the cold, hard, disgusting truth was that despite the promises nothing was even close to being okay. He went from having a happy mom, a house with a big yard, a school he liked and good friends, to living in a cramped apartment in the middle of one of the biggest cities he had ever seen.

The slow motion in which Jack seemed to be traveling as he replayed this string of broken promises ended as he was jerked back to reality by a large thud and the sharp ache of his body hitting the concrete. Laying there on the cold ground, Jack couldn't have asked for better proof that things were just as bad at school as everywhere else in his life.

Jack hated his school. No one wanted to be friends with the new kid. Worse still he had somehow managed, in just two short months, to become the favorite target of the school bully.

The name Charlie Bilson was dreaded by everyone who graced the middle school halls. A miserable human being, Charlie never missed an opportunity to ruin someone's day and no one seemed able to escape his mean tricks. Of particular interest to Charlie was anyone new which made Jack his favorite target.

Charlie wasn't original. Most of his taunts had been used by bullies for generations and included old-time favorites such as knocking books out of hands, the occasional slam against a locker, forcing his victims to smell his stinky armpit, and the rhyming of one's name with something nasty. But his favorite was the trip and fall. At this Charlie was a master. Moments before as Jack had attempted to walk across the lunch yard to go back to class,

Charlie seemed to have reached out of nowhere and stuck his

lunch tray in front of Jack's next step. Not seeing the tray, Jack

stumbled over it and went flying into the air. He failed to achieve

much height but the landing was hard. A bruise would definitely

be involved.

As Jack lay on the ground he knew the most important thing

he needed to do was to get up quickly and move into the build-

ing. Struggling to stand, Jack could hear Charlie taunting him.

"Whoa watch your step there Jacky boy," Charlie teased.

"Maybe Jacky needs glasses."

Jack could hear the laughs and jeers of his new classmates.

He had foolishly convinced himself that this was the worst things

could get when he heard it. Coming from across the yard, a lone

girl's voice began to shout, "Leave him alone Charlie." Riley Cald-

well had pushed herself up from the tree she had been reading

under and begun to march across the school yard towards Jack,

Charlie, and the gathering crowd of students.

While Jack's social awkwardness stemmed from being new

to school, Riley had grown up with these kids and had always been slightly on the outside. She was tall with long brown hair and clothes that were always a little on the wrong side of the latest trend. With her head constantly buried in a book, she always seemed to be by herself even when standing in a crowd.

To make things worse for Riley, there were many stories that circulated about her. As is the case with most middle school gossip, none were true; but it certainly didn't help her to blend in. Centering on why she had to live with her grandfather, the stories were as ridiculous as her parents being in prison; her parents not wanting her and leaving her with her grandfather before they ran off; and even that her grandfather was mean and kept her locked in her room after school so she wouldn't have any friends.

Jack had heard these stories about Riley. Being a new kid he was sure there were stories floating out there about him too. He didn't believe the gossip about Riley, but having enough of his own problems he had kept his distance from her as much as the other students.

Never one to blend in or go with the crowd, Riley decided to take action now as Jack lay on the ground. While everyone else was either looking away pretending the bullying wasn't happening or nervously laughing at Charlie taunting Jack, Riley stomped across the yard shouting, "Who do you think you are Charlie Bilson? Leave him alone."

"Oh look Jacky boy," teased Charlie. "Here comes your girlfriend weird Riley."

The truth was, if there was one person at school Charlie might be a little afraid of it was Riley. She wasn't tougher than him, but she never seemed afraid of him or to care what he did. Not wanting to engage with Riley but not wanting to look weak in front of the crowd of kids, Charlie shifted gears and, motioning to his crew, said, "Come on guys, Jacky boy's girlfriend's coming. Let's give the love birds some room." He laughed as he walked off, leaving Jack lying on the concrete.

"Are you okay?" Riley asked as she stooped down and offered her hand to try to help Jack up.

Jack should have been grateful. Riley was the only person since he had arrived at this school that had ever said hello or tried to be nice, but Jack was embarrassed and angry at the world at the moment and so instead pushed away her offered arm.

Stumbling first up onto his knees and then standing he said,

"Leave me alone! If I had wanted your help I would have asked for it. The last thing I need is the weirdest person at this school standing up for me. And even worse now everyone's going to think we're friends!"

Jack instantly regretted what he said. He saw the look of hurt on Riley's face but knew it was too late to take it back. "Okay," Riley said with a slight nervous laugh. "You've been having such a good time at this school that I'm sure you wouldn't want to ruin it by making a friend." She walked off and went back to the tree, grabbed her book, and headed into the school. Just then the bell began to ring signaling the end of the lunch period.

Jack wanted to call out and stop her. He wanted to apologize but he didn't. He was embarrassed, his knee had started to bleed from where he had skidded onto the pavement, and he just wanted to get back to class and get this day over as fast as possible. Although with the turn his life had taken he knew the next day promised to be no better.

On the walk back into school Riley cursed herself for getting involved. Why did she always think things would be different? She just hated boys like Charlie Bilson. Not for the first time she wondered what happens to someone to make them think it's okay to treat others the way Charlie did.

Riley knew she didn't fit in at school. She knew the crazy things people said about her. Whenever a new story would get started she would share it with her grandfather. Sometimes they would laugh together about how ridiculous it was. It's not that the stories didn't hurt, but sharing them with him always made her feel better.

Her grandfather was the nicest person she had ever known. He was kind and smart. They had always had a special but different kind of relationship. For as long as she remembered she had called him by his first name, Matthew. Maybe it was because in addition to being a grandparent to her, he had been playing the role of mother and father for most of her life. He had also opened up a whole new world for her with his care and support. But of course no one saw that. They just saw a weird girl who never seemed to fit in.

Jack's reaction to her offer of help had been a bit surprising and hurt more than she cared to admit. She had watched him struggle the past few months with being new in school. He seemed sad and a little lost and she could imagine how he was feeling. She didn't mean to get involved. The words just seemed to have flown out of her mouth. They usually did. Still, he didn't have to be so mean. The words stung anew as she replayed them in her mind…

*The last thing I need is the weirdest person at this school standing up for me. And even worse now everyone's going to think we're friends!*

If someone so new to school, who seemed almost as out of place as she felt, could think she was so weird that the worst thing would be that they might be friends, then there probably was no hope for her at school. Riley would just have to face the fact that she wasn't meant to have friends like everyone else.

Besides, the life that she and her grandfather lived sometimes made ordinary things like having a friend difficult. Still, it would have been nice to have even just one friend. The thought weighed heavy on Riley as she headed off to her next period class.

# Chapter Two

Walking home to his apartment after school, Jack thought about his mom and their recent move. His mom hadn't always been a mess, but after his father left suddenly when he was six his mom often seemed unable to hold things together. She had eventually tried to date again but it never worked out. Jack suspected she missed his dad more than she let on.

After his mom's boyfriend had decided to break up with her, things really seemed to fall apart and she seemed more than a little lost. It was Aunt Jane who had come to the rescue, encouraging them to move to New York City, and getting Jack's mom a steady job as a receptionist at her firm. It meant moving to a new, much bigger city. Jack's opinion about the move had not been asked. His mom now worked long hours, but she was slowly starting to come alive again. For that, Jack would always be grateful to his aunt.

As he walked into their apartment Jack was more than a little surprised to see his mom home. Immediately fearing the worst, he nervously asked, "What's wrong? Why are you home?"

"I can't just be home to see how my son's day went?" Jack's mom replied with a slight laugh. The truth was her son's constant unhappiness since their move had made her feel guilty and less able to connect with him than usual.

"No, not anymore," Jack replied more harshly than he had intended. "If we were at our old home and everything hadn't changed you would have been here, but not now."

Letting out a tired sigh his mother came over to Jack and put her arm around him. It had been a really long day and though he was trying to be tough, Jack let his mom hug him for a few seconds.

As Jack eventually pulled away, his mom said, "They called from the school and said there was an incident in the yard. They said you weren't hurt but that you wouldn't say what happened."

"It's nothing," Jack quickly replied. *I can't even escape this at home*, Jack thought.

"So that means you don't want to talk about it?" his mom asked. "Is there anything I can do?"

Anger swelling, Jack snapped and said, "Yeah, you could have not lost your job and you could have not made me leave all my friends to move to this stupid city where I have none. Everything is awful." Jack didn't mean to sound so angry. *Will I never stop hurting people?* he wondered.

Not seeming to mind the things he had just said, his mother simply replied, "Someday, Jack, I hope you'll realize I am doing the best I can."

Later that night, Jack lay in bed thinking about how awful the day had been. He hated his new school. He absolutely detested Charlie Bilson. More than anything though, he felt horrible about the things he had said to his mom. None of it was her fault. His mom had always done the best she could. She was great really.

For as long as he could remember it had been just the two of them. His dad had left when he was young so he didn't have many clear memories of him. His mom said he loved them but he traveled a lot, and one time while on a business trip he just never came home. Jack tried every once and a while to ask about his father. He suspected that there was more to the story than what his mom told him, but he knew she wasn't ready to talk about it. One day he would find out more but for now he was tired of thinking about it.

Riley also came into his mind. He knew she had only been trying to help. In fact, she was the only person at that school who had ever made an effort to be kind to him. It had taken nerve to stand up to Charlie Bilson like that and he had repaid her by being a jerk. These thoughts weighed on Jack's mind as he finally drifted off to sleep.

# Chapter Three

Sunshine streaming through the bedroom window wasn't the thing that woke Jack the next morning or any morning since he had moved to New York. The orchestra of city noises that surrounded him at all hours of the day and night were what first greeted Jack. Getting out of bed, he stretched and shuffled into the kitchen.

Expecting to find his mom and hoping to be able to apologize for his anger the night before, he found instead an empty apartment and a note on the kitchen table. Picking it up he read,

*Good morning Jack,*

*I know how hard this move has been for you. I'm sorry it feels like everything is upside down and it will never be right again. I promise you though it will. This is a new start for us and things will get better.*

*I know you wanted to say you were sorry this morning but there's no need. I'm your mom and I already know it.*

*I'm sorry we won't get to spend the day together but I got called to cover for someone at work. I left some money in the top desk drawer. You should go explore the museum today. I know that always makes you happy.*

*Be safe and I'll see you at dinner.*

*I love you,*

*Mom*

Jack had to smile. His mom always knew what he needed. She was right about the museum too. Since their move to the city, wandering the museum's corridors had been his one great escape.

One of his favorite things to do back home was to visit the art museum. He would get lost for hours looking at all the different works on view. For as long as he could remember looking at art had always made him happy.

So far the museums were the only good thing he could find about living here. There were so many different ones to visit. His favorite by far was the New York Museum of Art. It housed one of the world's greatest collections of art. Jack could and had

gotten lost for hours exploring gallery after gallery filled with art,

from ancient mummy tomb paintings to fantastical video light

displays.

Hurrying to get dressed, Jack stashed his sketch pad in his

backpack and headed out the apartment door. It was twelve

blocks to the museum and Jack knew the route by heart. He had

learned quickly how to navigate his way on both the city's bus

and subway systems, but on a day as nice as this Jack wanted to

walk.

On the few occasions Jack could forget the nightmares of

school and the fact that he had no friends, he could almost enjoy

the energy of this city. Eight blocks and the city street became

part of the park. No matter what time of day or night it was, the

park was alive with people. Sometimes he walked along the out-

side edge of the park looking at the street vendors selling every-

thing from ice cream cones to vintage record albums.

Today he chose to walk through the park itself. Saturdays

brought a mix of everyone from families out for strolls, to joggers

out for a morning run, to tourists taking photos with their cell phones. Jack took it all in on his way to the museum.

Visiting museums always made him think about his father. Having left when he was young, Jack had few clear memories of his dad, but the one he remembered best was of going with him to the art museum. His father left shortly after he started school, so he couldn't have been more than four or five when they would visit. Still, he often returned to a hazy memory of walking with him through the galleries and holding his hand while they moved from picture to picture. Whenever he would gather the courage to ask his mother about this she would say his father liked art and they had gone together to the museum a few times. She never elaborated on these visits, but Jack suspected they were somehow an important part of his childhood.

As always, Jack became excited when he caught his first glimpse of the museum. As he climbed the museum's steps he knew once inside he would be able to forget about his horrible week and spend his Saturday being transported to the other worlds that were to be found on the long, great expanse of the museum's walls.

Since his mother had bought him a membership he was

able to bypass the long line of visitors and move quickly into the museum space. Although the museum was huge, after his first few visits he no longer needed to use a map. During each trip he chose a new gallery and soaked up all its wonders, then returned to his favorite galleries before ending his visit.

It always amazed Jack how quickly time went by when he was in the museum. Hearing the low grumble of his stomach he looked at his phone and realized it was after 3 PM. He had been there for hours and he knew he'd better start heading back to his apartment. He wanted to make sure he was back in time for dinner so he could apologize to his mom.

Heading down the corridor leading to the main exit, Jack was just about to round a corner when he felt the sharp smack of impact. Stumbling back Jack said, "I'm so sorry."

"Oh, it's you," a voice said sounding surprised. Thinking the voice sounded familiar Jack looked up to see Riley Caldwell staring at him. She was rubbing her forehead.

A wave of embarrassment washed over Jack as he looked at Riley. He instantly went back to the moments when he had been so horribly cruel to her the day before. Simply put, he wanted the floor to open up and swallow him whole so he could just escape. Realizing that the likelihood of this happening was slim, he knew he would have to say something. Stumbling on his words Jack said, "I was looking at the paintings and I didn't see... I mean sorry I didn't... Are you hurt?"

"Not now," Riley replied.

Jack cringed at her words. He stood there staring at Riley as if seeing her for the first time. Everything about her was odd and mismatched somehow. She certainly didn't dress like the other girls in his class. Nothing she wore ever really matched and yet on her it seemed to fit perfectly. Today was no different. She was wearing a green cardigan over a grey t-shirt with a big black peace sign, black leggings, and red tie-up boots.

"Maybe you're the one who got hurt," she said, laughing.

Jack realized he had been staring. The truth was he was struggling to figure out what to say next. Knowing he had no choice but the truth, he took a deep breath and blurted out, "I'm really sorry about yesterday. I should never have said the things I did. I was just angry and embarrassed."

Riley stared at him for a few seconds. Then, shrugging her

shoulders she said, "Okay. Thanks. It was my fault. I shouldn't have butted in. Charlie Bilson is a real jerk but clearly no one needs my help."

"No, I really appreciated it," replied Jack, shifting nervously from foot to foot.

Laughing, Riley said, "Well then you're welcome. And don't worry; this doesn't have to make us friends or anything."

Jack looked pained. This apology was not going the way he had wanted it to and now he was making it worse.

"I'm just kidding. It's fine Jack. No hard feelings," Riley said, smiling. Looking down at her watch she added, "I really have to go but I'll see you at school." And with that Riley bounded down the hallway, disappearing into another gallery space.

# Chapter Four

The sight of Riley in school on Monday morning made Jack feel guilty all over again, but she was true to her word. She must not have had hard feelings because when they passed she smiled and waved hello. As Jack waved back he realized he liked how able Riley was to be her own person. She didn't fit in any better than he did. Jack at least tried to blend in and be as average as everyone else, whereas Riley couldn't help but stand out.

Later during lunch when Jack was sketching in his notepad, he heard a voice say, "So you're an artist too."

Looking up as Riley took a seat next to him, Jack quickly replied, "An artist? No. Not like the real ones anyways."

"It was kind of a surprise to see you at the museum. Did you have fun?" Riley asked.

"Are you kidding?" Jack replied, "It's the only good thing

about this city."

Riley laughed. "Yeah, well, I wouldn't necessarily agree with that, but it certainly is an amazing place. But do you really hate it here so much?"

"Oh no, I love it," Jack replied sarcastically. "I love being bullied by a gigantic moron, living in an apartment that is just a few hundred feet larger than my bedroom in my old home, and having no friends. It's been a real treat."

"Wow. Don't sugarcoat it or anything." Then, smiling, Riley stood up and said, "I better go. I don't want to risk people thinking we might be friends."

"Look, I'm really sorry," Jack started.

Riley laughed and said, "Relax Jack. I have to get to class, but who knows? Maybe the city won't turn out to be so bad. You might even make a friend or two."

As Riley walked away Jack had to smile. She didn't fit in any better than him but he honestly believed she didn't care. Jack knew he could use a friend. It was just not as easy to put himself out there again as it had been before. A friend, Jack had learned, was a hard thing to make and an even harder thing to keep.

# Chapter Five

On Friday morning Jack found himself at the museum again but this time as part of a school trip. Listening to the museum tour guide drone on about each painting, he couldn't help wishing he was off exploring the galleries on his own.

"This work, a depiction of Saint Anthony created with gold leaf, is typical of the fourteenth century icons found in churches of the period," the guide recited as if from a script. The class was in front of a display case filled with paintings, statues, and other bejeweled items.

Jack struggled to maintain his attention. *Seriously, anything would be more interesting*, he thought to himself. Looking around the room he spotted Riley. He had known she was on the trip but had been placed in the other tour group when their class had been divided. Now he watched her start to break away from the guide and make her way towards the gallery's entrance.

"You now have ten minutes to explore the Medieval rooms on your own before we move on to the Impressionist galleries," the guide said. "But remember we meet back here in ten minutes."

As the guide was finishing this reminder Jack saw Riley slip out the doorway and head down the gallery corridor. Without thinking, Jack began to move towards the door. Looking once over his shoulder to make sure no one saw him, he dashed out of the room.

He had no idea why he had done what he had. He didn't break rules. He hadn't said more than a few words to Riley since that day at the lunch table. But here he was following her down one corridor and through a sea of gallery rooms towards a back stairwell marked "PRIVATE."

He was debating what he should do next when Riley turned around and said, "So what's your plan now Jack?"

Suddenly embarrassed and a bit defensive, Jack answered back, "I didn't mean to follow. The tour was so boring. I just wanted to see where you were going."

Riley smiled and replied, "Okay then Jack the rebel, you can tag along but if we get caught you're on your own."

Jack must have looked a bit nervous because Riley laughed and said, "Don't worry Jack. I know where we're going and we can be back in plenty of time before they even think to miss us."

Jack was impressed following Riley as she maneuvered her way through the museum corridors as if she had done it a hundred times before. She didn't even hesitate as she pushed open a door marked "EMPLOYEES ONLY."

"I don't think we should be here," Jack said, pausing once they were through the doorway.

Just then a formal looking woman in a suit walked by, smiled, and said, "Hi Riley. Just couldn't stay on your tour could you? Matthew is down in the lab. It's been a busy day."

"Thanks Margaret," Riley replied and, grabbing Jack by the shirt sleeve, she asked, "Still worried we're going to get in trouble? Come on Jack. There's something I want you to see."

Jack gave up and just decided to follow her. Besides, he was having too much fun being behind-the-scenes at the museum to worry anymore.

After following Riley down two flights of winding stairs, they stopped in front of a door marked "CONSERVATION LAB." Riley pushed opened the door and walked into the room.

The room was full of painting supplies, frames, and stretched and rolled canvases. There were work tables littered with brushes, paints, and other strange tools. Paintings were stacked on the floor and leaning on easels. Jack recognized some of them as paintings he had seen before hanging on the museum walls.

"I had a sneaking suspicion you wouldn't make it through the entire tour," said a voice from somewhere in the corner of the room.

Laughing, Riley replied, "Now come on. You should be impressed I lasted as long as I did."

Jack had been so absorbed in looking around that he failed to notice the man sitting at the work table at the back of the room. He was older, with gray hair that had begun to recede, and yet something about him seemed young and energetic. The smock, faded jeans, and canvas sneakers he was wearing were covered in splashes of paint in a variety of colors. His glasses were made of a thick black frame and he removed them as he looked up to smile at Riley.

"I see you brought someone along in your escape," he said, smiling at Jack.

Jack was suddenly nervous that he wasn't supposed to be here and quickly said, "I'm sorry. I followed Riley and made her take me along."

"Now don't go making him nervous," Riley said, laughing, to the old man. "Jack this is my grandfather. He works here in the museum."

"So this is Jack," the man replied. Pushing away from the table and moving towards Jack, the man reached out, took Jack's hand in a firm shake, and said, "I'm Matthew. It's a pleasure to meet you, Jack. Riley has told me all about you."

"I don't know what she would have said," Jack started to ramble.

"That's enough now Matthew," Riley said quickly to her grandfather as she wrapped her arm around his shoulders and gave him a quick kiss on the cheek.

Jack didn't know what to react to first. He wondered just what Riley had said about him. He doubted any of it could be good. And why had she just called her grandfather Matthew? He couldn't imagine calling his mother by her first name. But as he watched the two of them it seemed the most natural thing in the world.

A bit desperate to change the subject, Jack quickly asked, "Do you really work here? It must be so cool to be so close to the art. Some of my favorite paintings in the world are in this museum's collection."

"I know," Matthew replied. "I've been here for many years and sometimes I still can't believe I get to work with these paintings."

"Matthew doesn't just work here," Riley said smiling. "He repairs the works when they get damaged or too old and need a bit of touching up. He's one of the few people in the museum who can actually touch the works. It's kind of amazing really."

"And you get to be here too? Wow," Jack said, more to himself than either of them.

"Jack," Matthew said smiling. "Would you like to see what I am working on right now?"

"Really? Yeah, that would be great!" said Jack as he walked with Matthew over to his work station. On the table was a stretched canvas painting of a vast blue ocean. In the foreground was a white sandy shore that seemed like it would stretch on for miles. Overhead a brilliant sun was shining down from the sky. "It's beautiful. Is this of some place real?"

"Good question," Matthew said. "This painting was done by a famous Dutch artist in 1742. It depicts somewhere in the Caribbean although we don't have any further specifics as to the actual location. The artist was known to have taken part in two expeditions to the Caribbean, during his life, and it is believed that he either painted the work while on one of the visits or made preliminary sketches of the island and used them to then create the painting at home in the Netherlands."

"Why are you working on this painting?" Jack asked, unable to take his eyes away from the canvas in front of him.

Moving his hand to the lower corner of the painting, Matthew said, "See this area here? After a certain number of years paint can start to crack and eventually flake off the canvas. This is especially true when the paint is thickly applied as this artist often did in his paintings."

"So you can fix the cracks?" Jack asked, totally absorbed.

"Yes, in a manner of speaking," Matthew replied. "Basically, you remove the flaking layers very carefully and then rebuild the painting layer by layer. You have to match the color perfectly and try to blend it to the original painting as closely as you can so that no one will be able to tell it has been worked on or that new paint was added."

"It must take a lot of time," Jack said.

"And patience," Matthew said smiling. "But I love my work."

Jack was so absorbed in the painting that he failed to notice the slight look of concern that crossed Matthew's face as he saw Riley staring intently at a painting propped against the back wall.

Crossing over to Riley, Matthew began a whispered conversation. Jack suddenly grew aware that Matthew was no longer next to him. Looking up, he thought he overheard Matthew tell Riley that she needed to be more careful.

Catching Jack's eye, Riley smiled and, returning with Matthew back to the work station, said, "Jack, we better go before someone realizes we're missing."

Matthew touched Jack kindly on the shoulder and said, "You will have to come back again with Riley when you aren't with your class."

"Thank you. I'd like that," Jack replied. Matthew now seemed so at ease that Jack felt he must have been mistaken to sense any alarm in the old man.

"See you later Matthew," Riley said moving them both towards the door.

"Thank you," Jack said again, as Riley led him out of the room.

Riley steered them with a sense of urgency back up the two flights of stairs and down many museum gallery corridors before they were able to merge back with their group. Luckily the class was in one of the dark video galleries. It was easy to blend back in without anyone noticing two additional forms joining the mass of students.

"So you liked being a rebel?" Riley whispered, leaning close to Jack.

"Be careful. People see us whispering in the dark and they might think we're friends or something," Jack replied smiling.

Riley elbowed him and laughed.

# Chapter Six

Riley and Jack became inseparable after the trip to the museum. Jack had missed having a friend. Riley, who had never really fit in, suddenly found that with Jack it was okay to just be herself.

While their friendship started over an interest in art and a visit to the museum, they soon realized they had a lot of things in common. They liked the same movies and books and of course they shared an intense dislike of Charlie Bilson.

After school and on the weekends Riley took Jack to explore different parts of the city. Because of her, he started to see how much the city had to offer.

They also spent time at each other's houses. Jack's mom liked Riley and Jack was crazy about Matthew. He loved to listen to Matthew talk about his work and the ways that he repaired the museum's paintings and sculptures.

Often after school Jack and Riley visited with Matthew in the museum's conservation lab. Jack felt special being able to go through the museum with Riley. Jack was able to watch how Matthew repaired the flaking paint on the ocean painting he had seen on his first visit to the lab. Matthew seemed to really enjoy explaining the steps of the repair.

Jack and Riley also shared similar family backgrounds. Both had suffered the loss of parents. Jack opened up about his dad leaving when he was young. Riley's parents hadn't walked away; they had died. Her mother had died when Riley was born and, according to her grandfather, her father had died in a car crash when she was three. What she knew about her parents was from stories told by Matthew. Riley had confided in Jack that she wished Matthew spoke more about them, but he rarely did. They had that in common too, as Jack shared with Riley his frustration in his mother's secrecy about his father. For both the not knowing was sometimes as hard as the actual loss.

Despite their blossoming friendship, Jack couldn't help the nagging feeling that Riley was hiding something. It was nothing she *did* exactly. Rather at times he felt she was on the verge of telling him something and then she would pull back. Sometimes he caught Matthew and Riley in whispered conversations. Once he had suggested he and Riley stop by the lab after school. They had done it many times before, but this time Riley had nervously and quickly told him it wouldn't be a good idea.

Jack had always wanted to ask Riley if something was going on but he didn't know how. Besides, he could have easily been imagining things, and he didn't want to look foolish in front of Riley.

Then, a few months into their friendship, something happened that made Jack know that he hadn't been imagining anything. That afternoon he had a dentist appointment and had to leave school early. He knew Riley would be with Matthew at the lab after school. Wanting to see them both he had arranged with his mom to stop there on the way home as she went off to work.

Jack had visited so many times before with Riley that the guards recognized him and let him go down into the lab without her. Pushing open the door to the lab he could immediately sense something was wrong. Matthew and Riley both turned

quickly to the opening door. Riley moved fast to block his entrance and pushed him back out into the hall corridor.

"What are you doing here?" Riley asked nervously.

He knew it was close to closing time but stopping by had never been a problem before. A bit annoyed he replied, "Jeez Riley,
relax. I was on the way home from the dentist and thought I'd see
if you wanted to hang out and work on our comics before dinner.
If you don't want to I can just go…"

Cutting Jack off, Riley said, "Sorry Jack. Of course that would
be great. I was just surprised to see you. Let's go back to my
apartment and we can work on them."

Still a little bit weirded out by Riley's quick actions, Jack
asked, "Okay but aren't we going to wait until Matthew is ready to
go?"

Almost too quickly Riley said, "Actually he just told me he
has to stay late tonight to finish a sculpture repair he is working
on. I was about to leave when you came in."

Moving towards the lab door Jack said, "Okay but let me just
say hi and then we can go."

"No!" Riley replied too quickly. Then as if realizing she was

not making sense she continued, "I mean he really has to finish. We can catch up with him later. You know what he gets like
when he's deep into a work. He gave me pizza money. We can
pick one up on the way back to my house and you can stay for
dinner. Your mom is working late anyways."

Still a little put off by what had happened Jack agreed and
they went back to Riley's apartment, ate pizza, and worked on
their comics. The rule was that Jack had to be home by 8 PM
on nights his mom worked late. Matthew still hadn't come back
from the museum when Jack left Riley's apartment at 7:40 PM.

As he walked home Jack couldn't shake the feeling that something was off. It was odd that Matthew would work that late. He
also wondered why it seemed that Riley was trying to keep him
out of the lab that afternoon.

# Chapter Seven

Jack didn't see Riley at their school lockers the next morning. She wasn't in their third period science class either. It wasn't like Riley to not let Jack know that she wasn't coming to school. All day Jack couldn't shake the nagging feeling that Riley was up to something. *We're supposed to be friends*, Jack thought. *Why won't she tell me if something is wrong? What if something's wrong with Matthew?*

When Jack got home that afternoon, a note from his mother on the table and a covered plate to be warmed up for dinner in the fridge confirmed that she had picked up a late shift and he had the evening to himself. Jack decided to call Riley and make her tell him what was up. There was no answer on her home phone or her cell. Then he sent a text:

*Are you OK? Call me. Jack.*

No answer.

He knew he shouldn't, but Jack was starting to get angry. *She could at least have answered the text*, he thought.

Around 6 PM Jack warmed up the food his mom had left him and ate it for dinner. After another hour and a half of waiting with still no message from Riley, Jack couldn't take it anymore.

Worried that something might really be wrong, Jack made up his mind to go back to her apartment and check on Riley. This meant ignoring his mother's 8 PM rule, but this was important.

Jack had learned that the closer you make a lie to the truth, the easier it is to get away with something. When Jack's mom took a late shift she got home around 10 PM. Knowing there was always a small chance that his mother would get home early and find him missing, he covered his tracks by leaving her a note stating he was worried about the next day's history test and needed to study with Riley. He said he was going to Riley's and her grandfather would put him in a cab if it was past 8 PM.

Simple and to the point, the letter was only half a lie since he was actually going to Riley's. Jack left the note on the table and walked out of the apartment building.

On the walk Jack thought about how he had been in Manhattan for five months, and thanks to Riley, he had really started to like the city. There was always something new to see. Sometimes he felt if he lived to be one hundred he would never see everything the city had to offer. He hadn't thought of where he grew up as a quiet place, but after living in this city he realized it was. There was a constant energy and noise to New York like a non-stop hum. Sometimes it was incredibly loud from all the street noises, horns, and building activity. Other times it was more of a low buzz, like the sound coming from the street lights outside his bedroom window late at night.

Today the city was giving off a medium hum as he walked to Riley's. The drive-time after the work rush was over, but people were still bustling about to get to evening activities. There was also a soft quality to early evening time that he really liked. It wasn't completely dark yet so all the lights gave off a soft hazy glow.

Jack was so caught up in these thoughts that he almost walked past Riley's apartment. She lived in an old brownstone building that had what Matthew called "real city character." The inside of their apartment was big and open with two bedrooms. It had lots of windows and a separate kitchen and dining room.

The apartment Jack shared with his mother paled in comparison. It was technically two bedrooms, although Jack was convinced his room was actually a walk-in closet that had been labeled a bedroom by the landlord to increase the rent. There was no dining room. His mom had placed a table in a corner of the living room and a counter in the narrow kitchen constituted what the landlord described as a "breakfast nook." Still, it was clean, had a few working windows, and was close to the subway which (Jack had learned) in this city meant everything.

Jack had asked Riley once about her apartment. She said that Matthew had always lived in New York and got the apartment when it was rent controlled. That meant that the rent he paid, half the rent for Jack's apartment, could never be raised.

Just then, as he was about to cross the street, he saw her. Shutting the apartment building door behind her, Riley went down the stairs and made a right, heading down the sidewalk.

Jack saw her first and quickly ducked into a storefront's doorway so she wouldn't see him. At first Jack was furious. *So she has been there and just didn't answer my text. I thought we were friends but I guess not.* Almost as soon as Jack thought those things he knew he wasn't being fair. He couldn't be sure, but he thought he caught a look on Riley's face that he had never seen before. She looked scared—and he had never known Riley to be afraid of anything.

*I wonder where she's going,* Jack thought. She was walking in the direction of the museum and Jack couldn't shake the feeling that the museum, Matthew, and Riley's expression were all connected somehow.

Jack knew he should go back. He would be busted if his mom did get home early and called Matthew to check up on him. Still he couldn't shake the feeling that Riley and Matthew were hiding something, or that more importantly something could be seriously wrong. So against his better judgment, he continued to follow Riley.

Doubts as to what he was doing began to weigh on Jack after a few blocks. *What am I doing? Riley has a right to be out and not tell me. She didn't say anything was wrong. Maybe Matthew is working late and she is going to meet him so they can walk home together. But then why didn't she answer my text? And why did Riley look so worried when Matthew didn't come home yesterday night?*

*This is crazy,* thought Jack. *Either I should call out to Riley, catch up to her and ask her where she's going, or I should go home.*

If Riley was going to meet Matthew it wasn't like Jack could go with her. The museum was closed by now. Jack knew he wouldn't be able to go in after hours. *I should just turn around and walk home. Riley will text when she can. She'll tell me about it tomorrow at school.*

Jack continued to walk to the museum despite the arguments raging in his head. He made sure to follow Riley from a distance. *This is ridiculous,* Jack told himself. *I am spying on my only friend. I'm following her like some character in a movie. How would I explain this to Riley if she sees me? What could I possibly say that won't make me seem absolutely crazy?*

When they reached the museum Jack was careful to stay a few feet back, hidden from view. Jack had expected Riley to wait by the staff entrance, since that was where they often found Matthew when they met him after work. To his surprise he was instead forced to follow Riley as she rounded the corner to the back of the museum's shipping area entrance.

Having become dark it was more difficult to be seen, but still Riley looked over her shoulder once to make sure no one was watching. Then to Jack's surprise, Riley crouched down, popped open the cargo window at the base of the loading dock door, and slid through.

Jack had no idea what was happening but he was now sure that something was wrong. *Where is Riley going? Where is Matthew? How does Riley know about this way into the museum and how often has she used it before?* Jack ran towards the loading dock, his mind racing.

Riley had put the window back in place but failed to secure it. This made it easier than Jack had imagined to follow her into the building. Although it was dark, there was enough light for Jack to figure out where he was in the museum. He had been behind-the-scenes in the museum so often in the last three months with Riley and Matthew that it was surprisingly easy to head towards the conservation lab. He couldn't be sure where Riley was going but it was his best guess.

Once inside, the confidence that had propelled Jack to quickly follow Riley started to fade as he realized that he had actually
just broken into the museum. He had no idea what he would say
or what would happen if he were caught by the museum security
so he just pushed forward as quickly as he could.

Jack's heart nearly stopped as he heard the footsteps of a
guard coming down the hallway on the way to the lab. Quickly
he spread himself out flat against the side of the stairwell. Holding his breath, he didn't let it out again until he heard the guard
disappear around the corner.

*If I make it out of here without ending up in jail I'm going to
kill Riley*, Jack thought. He was equal parts scared and angry but
he moved forward.

Whatever he might have guessed he would find, he could
never have imagined what was *actually* happening. In the far
corner of the conservation lab was the painting of the ocean
scene in the gold frame that Jack had seen Matthew working on.
What was unbelievable was the vibrating, swirling white light that
was emanating from the painting. The whole corner was awash
in light and there Riley stood with her left arm reaching toward

the painting.

As Jack made a move toward Riley he accidentally knocked over some canvases propped by the doorway. As they crashed to the floor Riley turned back to find Jack standing in the doorway, complete disbelief radiating from his eyes.

"What are you doing here?" Riley hissed.

"What am I doing here? What are you doing here? Riley what is this? What's going on?" Jack asked.

"You need to go!" Riley yelled. "Jack, I mean it. I can't believe I was so stupid and didn't see you following me. You need to go. I can explain later, but now you need to go!"

A slightly hysterical laugh escaped from Jack's lips as he started yelling back, "I am not going anywhere until you tell me what is happening here. This is nuts! What is this light? What is this Riley? What's happening?" Despite his questions Jack knew whatever she might say couldn't possibly explain what he was seeing.

There was a part of Jack that wanted to leave. He was clearly dreaming. It was just one of those really vivid, realistic dreams and he was sure he would wake up any minute. And yet another part of Jack wanted to know more so he found himself moving forward toward Riley and toward the light.

Riley was almost crying now as she said, "I just don't have time to explain this and I can't miss this chance. Just remember you gave me no other choice." With that she reached out to Jack and, grabbing him by the arm, pulled him forward with her into the picture's swirling vortex of light.

# Chapter Eight

Jack was surrounded by intense light and a loud buzzing. It reminded Jack of the sound of a dentist's electric toothbrush only if there were a thousand of them being used at one time. It felt like there was no ground beneath him and he was free falling into the light. The only anchor in this strange sensation was Riley's hand. He could feel it solid around his arm as the only connection to something real. He couldn't see or hear Riley, but as long as he felt her hand he knew she was there with him.

The tumble through the light ended as abruptly as it started with the hard thumping of Riley and Jack's bodies hitting the ground.

"Jack are you okay?"

Jack opened his eyes to Riley's face hovering over his. Jack was trying to understand what had happened as he muttered, "I just don't… I mean, what happened… There was light coming from the painting."

Struggling to get up Riley whispered, "Jack, you have to stand up and we have to move."

"No," Jack half yelled. "I'm not moving. I'm not going one step further until you tell me what is going on. Am I dreaming? This can't be real! What in the world just happened Riley? It's like one of those stupid science fiction comics you make me read."

As Jack was coming around he was becoming both more nervous and animated. Riley knew she was going to have to explain but she also knew there were things she had to do first—like getting them somewhere out of the open until she could get her bearings.

"Jack I know this doesn't make any sense and you probably even hate me right now but you have to trust me. I know what I'm doing. You need to stay calm. I will try to explain everything to you but it is not good for us to be out in the open until I figure some things out." Pleading, Riley continued, "Do you think you could at least move with me over to that outcropping of rocks?

Then I promise I will sit down and tell you everything as best I can."

Jack didn't know what to do. He just sat there staring at Riley until, pulling him up, she said, "Come on Jack. You need to move."

Jack knew he had no choice but to follow Riley. He hoped this was just some crazy dream and he figured the sooner he followed her the sooner the dream might be over. A part of him also knew that if this wasn't a dream he was going to need Riley's help. It was strange, but as he looked at her he realized while she did look nervous she didn't look surprised.

Looking around Jack saw nothing but water. Feeling the sand under his feet as he ran, he knew he was on some sort of beach but his brain kept screaming it was impossible. *Maybe that painting was just a doorway and we are back outside the museum. But why make a door like that? And what kind of bizarre doorway is made of swirling light? We are definitely outside, but where? If we are outside the museum we should be in Manhattan. But none of this looks like the city. Where are all the cars and the noise? Where are the people? Where is the museum? How can we be at the beach?* Jack's brain was starting to hurt from all his racing, unanswerable questions.

*This has to be some crazy dream that just seems incredibly real. There can be no other explanation.* It was too much. Jack couldn't think it through anymore. *But if this is a dream why does it seem so real?* His legs hurt from running and he could feel soreness where his knees hit the ground when he fell. *That doesn't happen in dreams*, he thought.

When they were about fifty yards down the beach they reached the outcropping of a formation of rocks. Riley came to an abrupt stop, grabbed Jack by the hands, and forced him behind the rocks. Now safely hidden from view, Riley sat down. Looking at Jack she began, "Okay. Let me try to explain what—" But before she could finish her sentence she felt a push of hands against her shoulders that forced her to lurch forward, almost falling into the sand.

Jack couldn't believe he had actually pushed her. All the adrenaline that had been pumping through his body, combined with the fear and unanswerable questions, had just taken its toll.

"Hey," Riley said pulling herself back up to her seated position against the rock. When she saw the mixture of confusion and anger in Jack's eyes she decided it might be best to let him speak.

"Sorry. I didn't mean to do that," Jack apologized. "Are you alright?"

"Yeah I'm fine," Riley said. She was about to try to explain when Jack cut her off.

"Good, because I didn't mean to push you, but you don't get to talk yet. You need to tell me what is going on right now. First we were in the lab, then the painting had that light, then we were falling, and then running. I mean what is going on Riley? I must be dreaming. I must be. This can't be real. No one goes through a painting. Where are we? Maybe it was those spicy tacos I ate today for dinner. Mom is always saying that hot stuff will make you have crazy dreams."

By this point Jack had committed to a full blown crazy ramble. Riley understood that this was all part of the process. Besides it gave her a little time to come to terms with what she had done. *Matthew is going to be furious*, she thought to herself. *I can't believe Jack followed me. I can't believe I didn't see him. I panicked. I was worried about Matthew. I thought the portal was closing and what if I never got another chance. This has never happened before. What if I can't find him? What am I going to do? How do I explain this to Jack? How was he even able to come through? We have never tried to bring someone in. I must have made it okay when I held his arm. How am I ever going to explain this?*

Realizing that she had begun a chain of unanswerable questions in her own head, Riley looked up to find Jack still rambling his questions out loud. *Okay,* she thought. *It is what it is and I need to get a grip and start doing what I came here to do. I will just need to explain it the best I can to Jack. After all, we are in this together now.*

Riley cleared her throat to make Jack pause in his rambling. Taking advantage of the brief silence Riley said, "Jack, um, do you think it's okay if I try to say something now?"

Jack let out an exasperated sigh and, rolling his eyes, said, "Fine."

Riley began, "I've never had to do this before. I mean, explain what just happened, so I don't know exactly what I'm doing.

Just do me a favor Jack because I know you will have questions but just wait until I'm done. I am afraid if I just don't say everything at once I won't be able to get it right."

Jack nodded and Riley continued. "I know you are thinking that everything that has just happened must be a dream because what other explanation could there be right? I promise you it is not a dream. This is real. As real as the two of us, our school, that bully Charlie Bilson, and the comic books we are working on together.

You didn't dream the vibrating light in the corner of the room. It was coming from the painting of the ocean shore Matthew had been repairing. Remember he was showing you the corner where he was working on replacing a part of the ocean's blue that had cracked and broken a bit?"

Jack nodded. For the first time since they had arrived he was quiet.

Riley continued trying to explain. "The swirling light coming from the painting provides a portal. It is a sort of pathway from our world into the world of the painting."

Jack started to shake his head and made a move to get up. Riley reached out and putting her hand on his arm to stop him she said, "Please Jack just wait. There really is no other option but to listen right now."

Jack reluctantly nodded and settled back down so Riley could continue. "I know what I've said sounds crazy, but I am telling you it's true. It's not like this is something that happens every day or to most people. I didn't believe it at first either when Matthew told me a few years ago. I was ten, we were in the museum's lab, and he said he had something important to tell me. He said he and I come from an ancient line of people known as art jumpers. Art jumpers have the ability to go into and out of paintings. We don't exactly know why or when it started. Each jumper has discovered it after first being drawn to viewing or working with art in some way. Some have been artists or dealers and others conservators like Matthew.

Once you know it's possible, the pull to go into a painting is very strong. Still we practice control and are careful to make sure we aren't discovered.

It's kind of like how when you read a book you can get transported to another place and time. You travel to a world sometimes completely unlike your own. That's what art jumping is like for us. It's a way to explore a different world for a bit and then come back home. The one big difference is that we don't just get to read about and imagine the world. We physically get to go.

There are rules that are passed down from generation to generation and I broke more than a few of them this evening. You should never have followed me you know. You had no right. What were you doing there anyway?"

"You mean I'm allowed to talk now?" Jack asked a bit more grumpily than he had intended. "Sure Riley. The absolute most important thing at this moment is for you to have your question answered about why I followed you to the museum. You just told me that while other kids might go to the movies or play video games for fun, you jump through paintings. And sure, we just happened to have traveled through a beam of light coming from a glowing golden picture frame and tumbled onto an ocean's beach somewhere we don't know where and we don't know when right? And I'm stuck here with you and who knows how this happened or if I will ever make it back, but please don't worry because I'll be sure to answer your question first."

Jack was on a roll again. He knew he should probably just calm down. Still what Riley was telling him seemed completely unbelievable and he was beginning to feel like he might not be able to breathe for much longer.

Jack so far had tried to comfort himself by thinking this had to be some crazy dream and that he would wake up soon in his bed in his apartment. But as Riley tried to explain he had this overwhelming sense that this wasn't the case. It felt too concrete to be a dream. Everything seemed too real. Acknowledging this Jack actually grew a bit calmer.

Pausing and looking straight at Riley he asked, "This isn't a dream is it?"

Riley who had begun to smile, said softly, "No Jack. I'm afraid it's not."

"We just went through a painting Riley," Jack said and then immediately felt silly for stating the obvious.

"I know Jack," Riley replied. "That's what I've been trying to tell you. Now I will answer any of your questions that I can, but maybe first you could tell me how you followed me."

Slowly Jack began to describe his tale of how he arrived at

the lab. "Everything seemed strange yesterday afternoon. You looked nervous when I came in and I could tell you were hiding something. I wanted to know what was going on. Then today you didn't come to school. Later when you still hadn't answered the text I sent you, I decided to go to your apartment. When I was almost there I saw you leaving and followed you to the museum. I saw you sneak in. That was really cool by the way. Then I followed you down to the lab where all this insanity started."

Riley couldn't help but notice how proud Jack was of his spying techniques. She knew he was calming down and this was good. Jack needed to be calm if she was going to figure out how to find Matthew and get everyone home. It was still a mystery how Jack could have gone into the painting with her. She worried whether she would be able to get him back out again but didn't want to tell him. She knew she needed to find Matthew. Hopefully he would be able to explain this and get everyone home.

"Riley are you listening to me? I asked where Matthew is and what happens next," Jack said.

"Sorry," Riley said, realizing she hadn't heard a word Jack had just said. "Listen I know that this is a lot to take in," Riley replied, "but we need to figure some things out and fast. This is different than any of my past jumps."

"Different how?" Jack asked.

"Jack, I've never jumped alone. Matthew has many times but he has never let me go by myself." Riley continued, "Matthew has been working on this painting of the ocean for a while. He liked it a lot and jumped in once a few days ago. He's always liked the water. You know we go out to Long Island sometimes on weekends to sit at the beach. He liked the fact that this was the ocean how it was almost three hundred years ago since the painting was created in the seventeen hundreds.

Yesterday afternoon he went back in. It's rare for us to jump more than once into the same painting but sometimes we have."

"Was that when I stopped by the lab and you wouldn't let me in?" Jack asked.

"Yes," Riley answered. "I'm sorry I acted so strange. Matthew was about to jump when you started to come into the room. The portal was on the verge of opening and I was afraid you would see the light. I guess that doesn't matter now since you know, but at that moment I knew we needed to get away from the lab.

Before you came I had tried to convince Matthew not to go back into the painting. I don't know why but I just had this feeling that he shouldn't jump just then. He said he wanted to go but that he would be out and home by the time I went to bed. Evening came and went and he never came home. I barely slept. By this morning when he still wasn't back, I was seriously worried. I couldn't think about going to school today. I wanted to be at the apartment when he finally got home. I didn't even see your text. I was too worried about Matthew. You saw me as I was heading to the museum.

Matthew never breaks his word. He always finds or calls me right after a jump to let me know that he is alright. When you saw me tonight I couldn't take it anymore and decided to go back to the museum. I knew the only thing I could do was go back into the painting and find Matthew.

I'm really scared Jack. Something's wrong I just know it. Matthew would never miss coming back from a jump unless something went wrong. When he didn't come back yesterday night it meant he missed the return portal. I waited all today just hoping he had got back and for some reason couldn't get home to me or send word. I knew that wasn't true though. The only possible explanation is that he missed the portal and now he can't come back on his own. I knew the only way to get Matthew back was to go in after him and find him. I was about to jump in when you saw me. Once the portal began opening I just panicked and took you with me. I'm sorry. I know I shouldn't have but I wasn't thinking clearly."

Jack saw the worry on Riley's face. He knew it was now his turn to be a good friend and help Riley figure everything out. He liked Matthew and if the old man was in trouble or hurt somewhere he wanted to help.

"Riley," Jack began, "I know this isn't how I expected my evening to go but I know it's going to work out. We are going to figure this out together. We are going to find Matthew and then somehow, and I can't believe I am going to say this, but then we are going to go back through a painting or whatever happens next and we are all going to get back home. Let's start with where we really are and what we know."

More than ever Riley was glad she had met Jack and tried to help him that day against Charlie Bilson. She was glad she finally had a real friend and she was glad it was Jack.

As they continued to talk they began to look around and take inventory of their surroundings. The painting in which they had jumped had only depicted a small portion of the beach with a large expanse of ocean filling up most of the painting's canvas. The water, just as in the painting, was a bright clear blue. The sun was shining and it was hot.

The little stretch of beach visible in the painting had expanded far beyond the confines of the canvas. The beige, sandy beach went on for as far as they could see in either direction. Unlike in the painting, now they could see green visible beyond the interior edge of sand. It was nothing like the green you see in the park or the trees in New York. The island brush was composed of palm trees and other big tropical plants with glossy, wide leaves. The brush was dense and provided no clue about what lay hidden inside. The sounds of Manhattan, such a part of their everyday lives, were replaced on the island by a gentle quiet punctuated by the sound of the ocean waves lightly meeting the line of the sandy beach.

"You said this painting was made in the seventeen hundreds,

right?" Jack asked.

"Yes," Riley replied, "I remember Matthew saying it depicted a beach somewhere in the Caribbean. Unfortunately I don't
know much else about it. I wish I did, but I always kind of just
liked the view."

"Okay. A painting from that long ago," Jack began, "means
that this island will have no electricity or power at all. If we don't
know where we are then we don't know who else, if anyone, is on
this island. We don't know anything about what is out there or
more importantly where Matthew might be."

"I think we just start looking for Matthew. We need to find
him and get back," Riley answered, sounding nervous.

"I'm still trying to wrap my head around the fact that a few
minutes ago we left the museum and now we are literally in a
painting of an ocean some hundreds of years in the past," Jack
said. "I'm still not completely convinced I'm not dreaming, but
in case I'm not we better make a plan. I know you want to find
Matthew. We will, but I think that first we need to have a plan of
action."

A small smile crept over Riley's face, and while she was still highly anxious, she relaxed just a small bit. "Well look who's ready to take charge now," Riley said as she playfully pushed Jack on his shoulder—much lighter than he had pushed her a while back. As Jack laughed she continued, "Okay. First we need to get a better sense of where we are and where Matthew might have gone."

"When you jump a second time in the same painting do you land in the same place?" Jack asked.

"Yes," Riley replied "so that means Matthew landed right where we did on this beach during his two jumps."

"Riley how much time do we have here? I mean how does it work when you want to leave a painting?" Jack asked. "I think it might help in figuring out how to make a plan. Also I'd like to know how we are going to get home."

"The rule with jumping is that once you are in a painting you have eight hours," Riley began to explain. "Matthew would have had eight hours on the island before he had to make it back to the portal. Eight hours after you land the frame reappears. You have exactly ninety seconds to jump into the portal while it is open or it closes."

Jack looked at Riley and asked a bit nervously, "What happens if you don't make it to the portal on time? What happens if the portal closes and you aren't through?"

Looking away from Jack as if she desperately needed to focus on something down the beach, Riley paused before she softly spoke. "It's gone, Jack. Once the portal closes it doesn't reopen."

"You mean you're trapped?" Jack asked.

"Yes," Riley answered. "The portal won't come back again unless or until another jumper comes into the painting. That's what we just did and now we have eight hours to find Matthew and jump back through the portal to get home.

Every jumper knows that you need to start your watch the minute you land through a portal. It doesn't matter what time of day is depicted in a painting. A jumper uses the time on his or her own watch as the guide to keep track of the time spent in a painting. It was the first thing I did after we fell on the beach. As of this minute if we don't reach the portal in seven hours and thirty-four minutes we are stuck here too."

Jack felt like he was going to throw up but fought the urge. He knew they needed to stay focused. Trying to draw up courage he wasn't sure he had, he said, "Okay then Riley. We will just have to find Matthew and get back to this beach to get into that portal in eight hours. I've been thinking. The sun is already starting to drop a bit in the sky. Eight hours means it is going to get dark and then just start to get light again before we get out. We have no idea where Matthew went but he would have started from the same spot we did. So I think two things are the most important to think about first. One, we need to start looking for any signs of Matthew beginning at the spot we landed. Two, we need to figure out what we are going to do to get by for the next eight hours."

"I've never spent much time camping or anything but I know we are going to need some food and shelter before it gets dark," Riley said. "I remember learning in school once that you can't drink water from the ocean because of the salt."

"Lucky for you," Jack said smiling, "that I've got a full water bottle in my backpack. It's not much but it will at least get us through the next eight hours if we only take little sips."

Riley hadn't noticed the backpack until now. She could have hugged Jack she was so relieved. "You know Jack you might be better suited for art jumping than you think."

Jack laughed and said, "You know this would actually be a really cool way to spend an afternoon if I wasn't completely freaked out about finding Matthew and making it home without being stuck in a painting for the rest of my life. It still seems more than a little unreal that we are in a painting."

Knowing just how Jack was feeling Riley said, "Sometimes I still can't believe this myself. But we can't focus on that right now. Since we have your water, let's start looking around. You don't have any food in that magic backpack do you?"

"Just some carrot sticks I didn't empty from my lunch bag when I got home from school," Jack answered. "At least it's something but we should definitely try to find some more food to eat if we can."

Moving out from the rocks, Jack and Riley started to head back towards the beach. Riley felt the need to explain a bit more and so continued, "One of the rules when we jump is we try to stay away from people we might encounter in the painting's world. We try to keep a low profile and make as little impact on the world as possible. It doesn't seem like anyone's around but we should be careful. The portal drop happened in the most wide open part of the beach so we needed to get away from there quickly. We need to try to get to a more covered, less visible area."

As they walked Jack and Riley tried to take in as much of their surroundings as possible. It was warm to the point of being truly hot. Staying in the shade was going to be important. The hotter they became the thirstier they would get, and they were going to have to be really careful with the little water that they had in case they couldn't find any other source while they were in the painting.

As they reached the place where they had been thrown to the beach, they saw the imprints their bodies had made in the sand. There was nothing else nearby. They hadn't really expected to see a set of Matthew's footprints but they had hoped.

"How are we ever going to find him?" Riley asked.

"I don't know," Jack answered, "but I do know we shouldn't waste time worrying. We just need to keep moving forward. So if there aren't any clear markings showing us Matthew was here, it means he could have gone in any direction. You know your grandfather better than anyone else. Look around and see if there is anything that might lead you to think he went in a certain direction. I know it's not as good as footprints but it's all we have to get started."

Riley knew Jack was right and they would need to stay focused. She began looking around and once more took in the whole view of the island, this time from the point of their landing. The beach stretching clear out for miles in either direction along the edge of the ocean offered no clues. She tried to think like her grandfather and knew that he too would have wanted to get away from the open view as soon as possible. The rocks would have provided a clear starting point because of the cover they offered. Yesterday would have been his second jump however, so he would have been a bit more familiar with the island and maybe wouldn't have needed the safety of the rocks after landing again.

Excitedly Riley grabbed at Jack's arm and said, "Look. See that thick patch of palm trees and bushes? There are coconut shells on the ground. That means someone has been there recently and the shade of those trees and how they lead into the island forest would have been as good a place as any for Matthew to start to explore."

Jack and Riley ran quickly across the beach and over to the palm trees. When they reached the spot they found that the sand there was littered with the fragmented remains of two coconut shells. The sight of the shells offered no concrete proof that Matthew had been there, only that *someone* had. Not wishing to focus too long on what that could mean or worry about who they might encounter if the coconut eater wasn't Matthew, Jack and Riley began to search the surrounding area. As they moved a bit further down into the vegetation they noticed a change in the branches that allowed a lightly worn path to come into view. They could see that the path led deeper into the island.

"I don't know if Matthew was here," Riley reasoned, "but if it was Matthew and he saw this trail his curiosity would have led him to follow it."

"Since we don't have any better guess as to where Matthew might have gone," Jack reasoned, "maybe we should follow the path."

Looking around her one last time, Riley nodded. "Sounds

like as good a plan as any, and besides we're going to need to find more protected shelter when the sun goes down. Deeper into the island sounds better than being out in the open on the beach."

# Chapter Nine

Together Jack and Riley began to follow the trail. They were careful to stay on it so as not to get lost. They knew it would be vital to easily be able to find their way back to the beach before the portal reappeared, and if they wandered too far from the trail that might not happen.

If the situation had been different and Jack and Riley weren't racing against the clock to find Matthew and get back to the portal in time, they would have had fun just exploring the island. There was a richness of plants filled with flowers in colors so vibrant that they had never seen anything like it before.

Jack remembered a school trip back home before they moved that he had taken to a rainforest habitat at the zoo. It reminded him a little of what he was seeing on the island but here there was so much more. As they walked the path, animals would appear and then scurry away as if they were playing an elaborate game of

hide and seek. Birds, large and small and of many different col-

ors, flew above their heads as they chirped to each other in their

own secret language.

"Jack, look!" Riley exclaimed. As Jack looked in the direction

of Riley's finger he saw a group of tiny monkeys springing from

tree to tree. Chattering away to each other, they barely seemed to

touch one branch before they were hurling themselves towards

the next one. Sometimes one of the monkeys would reach out

to grab the tail of one of the other monkeys more firmly planted

in the tree. Using the tail like a rope, the monkey would propel

itself forward to the next tree. "There's so many of them. It looks

so fun," Riley said, laughing out loud at the comical sight.

"It's amazing, isn't it?" Jack asked. "It reminds me of the

rainforest habitat at the zoo back home. I don't know whether I

should mention this right now but while we did see a lot of cool

animals at the habitat, there were also some more dangerous

looking ones."

Almost before he finished the words there was a large rus-

tling from the bush and a loud echoing sound that was half

squeal, half snort. Both Riley and Jack whipped around to their left towards the sound just in time to see a huge, wild boar come charging at them. It looked kind of like a pig but much larger with brown skin and wild unruly tufts of hair sticking out at all angles. Its snorting became louder the closer it came to their position on the path.

"Look out!" Riley yelled, pushing Jack to the ground right before she dove out of the way. Jack slightly raised his head just seconds before the boar charged through the gap their bodies made as they lay on the jungle floor. He was close enough to feel the beast's hot, stinky breath on his cheek.

"Did you… I mean that thing just…" Riley stammered.

"I saw its eyes Riley," Jack said in a hushed whisper as he got back up on his feet. "It was scared and it was definitely running from something. I think we better keep moving."

"You don't have to tell me twice," Riley said as she took Jack's hand to help her get back up. "Wow. That thing stunk."

"I thought nothing smelled worse than the time Charlie Bilson held my face into his sneaker in the gym locker room," Jack said with a kind of nervous little laugh, "but that thing more than stunk. It was putrid."

Neither Jack nor Riley had verbally agreed to increase their pace, but as they set out again they were definitely moving more quickly. Still careful to stick to the trail, they each kept a watch out for anything that might give them a clue about Matthew.

The sun was beating down and both Jack and Riley were starting to feel the fatigue from trying to move in the blistering heat. Jack was just about to suggest that they each take a sip of the water when Riley yelled out, "Jack, look!"

Focused on the path ahead Jack had not yet seen the solid formation of rocks about fifty yards east of the trail. The massive structure was partially hidden by some trees but a small part of the rocks was visible through the brush.

"It looks huge," Jack said. "Maybe we should go check it out."

Riley cut him off saying, "Shhh. Wait a minute. Listen."

"It sounds like water," Jack said, straining to hear. "We need to go see."

As they were about to head off the trail, Jack suddenly stopped Riley. "Wait. We can't lose sight of this path or we might not make it back to the beach."

"I've got an idea," Riley said. She took the bright purple belt she had been wearing and tied it high up around the trunk of a tree at the edge of the path. "It's bright enough to see from a distance. It will lead us back to the path if we get lost."

"Who says fashion can't be helpful?" Jack asked, laughing. "Come on. Let's go see where that water is coming from."

It didn't take long to reach the rocks. Once there they realized that the rocks were actually the back of a cave. The entrance on the opposite side was hidden behind a rushing waterfall. Beneath the falling water was a deep pool of crystal blue water.

"It's beautiful," said Riley.

"I don't think I've ever seen water so blue," Jack said. "I keep thinking of the colors in the painting. At first the colors seemed so real, but now I realize the artist hadn't come close to capturing the true blue of the ocean."

As a slow smile crept across her face Riley asked, "Do you think the water's cold?"

"Don't even think about it," Jack said, beginning to realize what thoughts were lurking behind her smile.

"I'm just saying it's so hot and we need to keep our energy

levels high if we are going to keep on looking," Riley answered. "What better way to stay cool? Besides it was just an idea."

"I guess it's not such a bad way to cool down," said Jack and before Riley saw it coming he placed his hands on her shoulder and back.

"Jack don't you dare—" Riley had no chance to finish her sentence before she was pushed and went crashing into the water with a loud splash.

Seconds later she broke through the surface, sputtering and spitting out water. Seeing the shock on Riley's face Jack began, "Now don't get mad, I just thought it—"

Riley's yell cut him off. "Jack you have five seconds to get off that rock and into this water or you'll live to regret it. One, two, three..."

Before she could finish Jack cried out, "Four, five!" and then jumped, cannonball style, into the water. As he bobbed up from under the water Jack looked at Riley and they both burst out laughing.

The water was icy cold at first but the warmth of the island sun made their bodies adjust quickly Within a minute Jack and

Riley were both swimming around splashing each other.

After about twenty minutes they found themselves at the water's edge. All of a sudden Riley grew serious again and quietly asked, "What if we can't find Matthew?"

Jack, trying to stay hopeful for Riley's sake, said, "We will. We have to and we will."

"It's as simple as that?" Riley asked.

"No," Jack answered, "but the way I look at it this afternoon I was looking for my friend who hadn't bothered to text me all day, and now I have jumped through a painting and am swimming in the pool of a waterfall. If all that can happen then I can certainly believe that somehow we will find Matthew and all get out of here. I can believe it and so can you."

Riley wiped at a tear that had started to trickle down her cheek. "Thanks Jack," Riley answered. Laughing she added, "You're a good friend and I forgive you for pushing me into the water."

"As long as I'm forgiven," Jack said, laughing. "Let's get out of this water and check out the cave. It might make good shelter if we need to find cover after it gets dark."

Once out of the water it was a short climb up the rocks to the cave. The closer they got to the entrance, the wetter it became. They needed to use each other for support to be steady enough not to slip.

The waterfall acted like a curtain over the cave's opening and Jack and Riley felt the spray of the flowing water as they went behind the waterfall and into the cave's entrance. Once inside they were grateful to the sun that was filtering into the cave not only because it was helping to start to dry their wet clothes, but also because it allowed them to see into the cave.

"It's a lot smaller than I thought it would be," Jack whispered to Riley.

"I'm thinking that's a good thing," Riley answered. Then seeing the questioning look on Jack's face she added, "This way if we can see to the back of the cave we can be sure there are no animals or anything else in here with us."

"Except for maybe a bat or two," Jack said, smiling.

"Don't even think it," Riley warned. She had shared her fear of bats with Jack when they had gone to the zoo one Saturday a few weeks ago.

Laughing to himself, Jack began to explore one side of the cave while Riley searched the back corner. Thinking it might come in useful, Jack put in his backpack a sharp rock he found on the cave floor.

"There looks like ash here," Jack called out. "Someone was here not too long ago and must have lit a fire."

On her way to check out the ash, a glittering flash caught Riley's eye. "Oh no," she cried out.

Running over Jack asked, "What's wrong?" He didn't have to wait for the answer. Riley was holding a pair of glasses that looked remarkably like Matthew's. Perhaps more alarming was the fact that the right lens had a large crack as if they had been stepped on.

"They're Matthew's," Riley stated in alarm.

"Are you sure?" Jack asked. "They look like his but can you be sure?"

"See here," Riley said showing Jack the glasses. "These glasses have the same blue paint smudge on the inside right frame as Matthew's pair. Something has to be really wrong. Matthew always wears his glasses. Even if he had broken them on accident he wouldn't have just left them. He needs to wear them. What if he just wandered off and is lying hurt somewhere?"

"Riley I know this is hard but we both need to stay calm," Jack said hoping he sounded reassuring. "Let's focus first on the fact that if these are Matthew's glasses than we know he was here and we know we are closer to him than we were a few minutes ago. We are going to find him. We just need to think."

"Okay," Riley said. "You're right. He was here. That's good, but Jack, he wouldn't have just left his glasses. So that means something has gone wrong."

"I think you must be right," Jack answered. "So now we need to figure out where he might have gone or what is wrong. Let's finish checking out the cave to make sure there aren't any other signs as to what happened to Matthew."

A close inspection of every inch of the cave resulted in no other clues. "Since Matthew wouldn't have just dropped his glasses it means something must have happened in this cave." Jack was clearly thinking things through as he spoke.

"There's no sign of a struggle and there is no blood, so maybe he hasn't even been hurt," Riley stated out loud, more to herself than to Jack.

Since Jack had come to New York and started at his new school he had tried hard to stay invisible. After he became friends with Riley he had a partner. She was a friend who made everything less lonely. Matthew had accepted him into their family and seemed happy to spend hours talking about art with him and showing him his work. Jack wasn't sure how it was going to happen but he was sure of one thing: he and Riley were going to figure this out, find Matthew, and get home before the portal closed for good.

Looking at Riley he asked, "Remember the cop movie we watched last Friday night at your house?"

"Yeah," Riley said, not sure where Jack was going with this.

"So before they could solve the crime they talked things through step by step," Jack continued. "I think that's what we should do."

"I like it," Riley said. "Let's review all we know right now."

"Okay," Jack said. "So what do we really know for sure? We need to start at the beginning, Riley."

Following Jack's lead, Riley began, "We know Matthew

jumped through this painting for a second time two days ago."

"And we know he didn't make it through the portal to return," Jack continued.

"Right," Riley responded, "because he didn't come home. Then we know where Matthew landed and we think he ate those coconuts and headed down the trail."

"We also know for sure that Matthew was here in the cave," Jack continued.

"Right," said Riley. "Finding Matthew's glasses is the first clear sign that we are on the right track. Matthew was here. But something had to have gone wrong because he wouldn't have just left them."

"So," Jack reasoned, "if something went wrong, Matthew had to have left this cave without the glasses. We didn't see any sign of someone being here on the way up to the cave. I think we should look on the other side of the cave and see if there are more clues."

"Okay," Riley agreed. "I don't want to imagine what happens if we don't find Matthew before it gets dark, but it's good we have this cave to stay in for shelter if we need it later in the evening."

Riley grew suddenly quiet and then, beginning again said, "Jack, we need to make sure we don't forget to watch the time. We have six hours and seventeen minutes left until the portal appears."

"Six hours," Jack muttered. "Six hours to find Matthew, get back to the portal, and get home. We might even have time for another swim and some sightseeing." Jack smiled at Riley.

Riley smiled back. Neither one would admit how scared they were that this wasn't going to work, but they both knew the only thing they could do was keep going.

# Chapter Ten

Riley was glad that Jack had followed her and she was forced to take him on the jump. Otherwise, she would have been alone on this island. That thought was more than she could handle right now. Knowing that she needed to focus on finding Matthew she said, "Let's go look on the other side of the cave. Maybe we'll find something that will let us know what way Matthew went."

The rocks were less slippery as Jack and Riley moved away from the waterfall. The path didn't offer any clues, but as they were scaling down the trail they heard voices in the distance. Riley and Jack froze. They had thought they and Matthew were the only ones on this island. They had never seriously considered that there might be others.

"Quick! We need to hide," Riley said as she grabbed Jack by

the arm and pulled him down behind a gap in the rocks by the side of the waterfall's cave. Neither said a word, but both were afraid the sound of their breathing and their hearts beating in their chests would get them discovered.

"We need to look," Jack said. "I think we have enough cover from the rocks to look out on the trail." Moving in silent agreement Jack and Riley quietly crept up the slightest bit to peer out over the rocks. Two men were coming down the path. They were dressed in dirty, ragged clothing. One was short and wiry with a bald head, while the other was tall with big muscles and a long black ponytail. They looked mean. Both were engaged in a heated conversation and were yelling and gesturing wildly. The tall man was dragging a dead boar behind him.

Careful not to be overheard Riley quietly said, "I never thought we were anything but alone on this island. Do you think that's the wild pig that chased us before?"

"I don't know but I'm thinking that's an awfully big pig for just two people to eat," Jack answered back. "There's got to be more of them."

"They don't look very friendly Jack," Riley said, worried.

"What if Matthew ran into them and something happened?"

"I know," Jack answered as worry crept into his voice despite his best efforts to keep it away. "I think we need to follow them and take a look."

Riley nodded. "But we need to make sure we stay back a bit. The last thing we need is for them to see us."

Walking as quietly as they could, Jack and Riley crept along the path at a good distance from the two men. "You know what this reminds me of?" Jack asked. "It reminds me of when I followed you as you broke away during our class visit to the museum."

Riley smiled, "Yeah who would have known you would have needed to use your rebel skills again so soon?"

Jack smiled back. Despite being completely scared, they kept creeping along at a good distance from the men. Twice they were nearly discovered, but were able to sneak back into the cover of the brush in time.

After ten minutes the men's walking began to slow down and it was then that Riley and Jack heard other voices. They watched as the men went off the trail, cut through the bush, and went back onto the beach. They must have been much further down from where they had landed hours before.

Jack and Riley slowly crept up to the bush and looked out onto the beach. Along the wide expanse of sand there were a few clusters of rocks similar to the one they had used as cover after landing through the portal. There were also five makeshift tents. Fires were glowing and there were other pigs already roasting over the fire pits.

"I count seventeen men," Riley whispered to Jack.

"They're real pirates. Look over there," Jack pointed left where a huge ship was moored out about five hundred yards from the island shore. All that was missing was the flag with skull and crossbones like in the movie version of every pirate ship.

"Riley, when was this painting created again?" Jack asked.

"I think it was sometime in the 1740s. I can't remember the exact year," Riley answered.

"Pirates were a real danger on the open ocean hundreds of years ago," Jack began. "I remember reading once about how pirates would anchor on certain islands as their base and then go back out onto the water to attack other ships and steal all their goods. This island might be one of their bases."

The presence of the pirates had made their entire jump much more dangerous. Jack had a sick feeling in his stomach as he said, "Riley these are bad people. They can't know that we are here. We need to find Matthew and get off this island."

"Oh no," Riley cried out. "Look!" As Jack turned he saw what had caused Riley's outburst. Matthew was sitting against the back of a rock near one of the fires. His hands and feet were tied and a cloth was stuffed in his mouth so he couldn't speak. He had a bruise on his head and the left sleeve of his button down shirt was ripped and hanging off his shoulder. He didn't look great, but he seemed to be awake and more importantly alive.

Unable to bear what she was seeing, Riley jumped up and began to push through the edge of the brush. "Riley, wait!" Jack cried as loud as he could without drawing attention. Grabbing her hard he pulled her back down towards him and into the cover of the brush.

"Let me go!" Riley struggled to get free. "We need to get Matthew."

"Riley listen to me," Jack begged. "There is nothing I want

more than to get Matthew to safety and get off this island, but we can't just go charging the beach. These are pirates. We are two twelve year old sixth graders from New York City. We can't rescue your grandfather from a band of pirates without a plan."

Riley knew what Jack was saying was right and they were going to need to stay calm if they wanted to succeed. They stayed hidden and took the time to observe the pirates on the beach. The seventeen men were of various sizes and strengths. A few didn't seem to be working very hard at all. They appeared to be both a bit fat and lazy. Most of the men, however, were busy with various labors. They were strong and more than a little scary looking.

As they watched the men it became clear that there was one pirate who was in charge of all the others. Tall, with strong muscular arms, he had a long red scarf tied around his head and he wore a gold hoop earring in his right ear. It was easy to tell he was in charge by the way he directed the actions of the other men. When he spoke they listened. At his command a few men were beginning to prepare the pigs for dinner, while others were busy moving things around the island.

There was also activity happening in the water. Riley and
Jack counted three men on the anchored ship. They were loading items from the ship down onto two rafts. Once loaded with
goods the rafts were brought back to shore. Four men were in
charge of each raft. Each man held onto a corner with a rope
as they swam towards the shore with the loaded raft. When the
water was shallow enough they would stand and pull the raft the
rest of the way to the shore.

A crew of pirates was waiting at the shore to unload the rafts.
The goods were then taken to be stashed in some hidden spot
behind the rocks on the beach.

As they watched, Jack and Riley saw that the process was
then repeated in reverse. Other goods and supplies, which must
have been hidden on the island, were loaded onto the raft and
brought to the ship for when they were ready to set sail again.

"I bet the things they are loading on and off the rafts are stolen goods from other ships," Jack said.

"If that's true then when they saw Matthew on the island they
might have thought he was here to steal the goods himself or that
he might tell someone else of the treasure they had stolen," Riley

reasoned to Jack.

"There is no way Matthew would have been able to explain why he was on the island," Jack began. "You're my friend and if you told me before today that you jump into paintings I would have thought you were crazy."

As they were talking they tried to keep their eyes on Matthew. Riley was concerned at how old and scared her grandfather looked. "We need to get him home," Riley said to Jack. "I can't lose him. He's all I have."

"I know," Jack said. He knew what it felt like to not have a parent. Suddenly his thoughts turned to his mom and how much she did for him. "You know you have me too Riley. You are the best friend I have ever had and the best thing to happen to me since we moved to the city. Matthew means a lot to me too. He's been so kind to me. I don't want anything to happen to him either."

"I know," Riley smiled back at Jack. "Listen I've been thinking about the pirates. There are too many of them and we are too far away from Matthew to ever make it to him, untie him, and get him safely away without being discovered. We need to shift something so the chances of success are more in our favor."

The sun began to set making its gentle transition from day to evening as Jack and Riley continued to observe the scene on the beach. With the fading sun the pirates began to slow down. As the work stopped the partying began. The pigs had finished roasting and the crew began to sit down to prepare to eat. As bottles of drink began to be passed around, the whole crew seemed to relax.

As they watched, two things became clear. Jack said, "I think this will go on for the night and there might be a way to make this work for us."

"I know," agreed Riley. "It's already 11 PM according to my watch. In a few hours I bet all these men will be out cold, sleeping off their partying. Right now there's no way to reach Matthew without being seen. But if everyone is sleeping…"

"They won't be able to see us," Jack said, excitedly finishing Riley's sentence. "In a couple hours after they have hopefully all fallen asleep," Jack reasoned, "will be our best chance of getting to Matthew undetected."

Riley looked at her watch then said, "We have a little more

than five hours until the portal returns. It's scheduled to appear on the beach where we first dropped in at 4 AM tomorrow morning."

"We need to wait a few hours," Jack said, his eyes twinkling with the start of a concrete plan. "Then we make sure the pirates are asleep and we move in and rescue Matthew."

Picking up on the plan, Riley continued, "We sneak in, untie Matthew, run off through the brush to the other side of the island, and wait until the portal appears."

"It's a tight time period," Jack finished, "but with a little luck I think we can make it."

# Chapter Eleven

Riley and Jack moved a bit further down into the island brush. They knew they were in for a few hours of waiting until the pirates were full and drifting off to sleep. They were still close enough to the beach, but now they would be able to better talk through their plan without the fear of being overheard.

Underneath the excitement about the hopes for a new plan, both knew that this was the only chance they had of getting to Matthew and making it back to the portal. If they missed the portal they were stuck. Unlike what they had done for Matthew, there was no one left to rescue the three of them if they missed the portal tomorrow morning. As if by some unspoken agreement they did not share this fear out loud.

Still, it was weighing heavy on their minds when Riley said, "I just wish there was a way we could let Matthew know we are here. He must be so scared that he is going to be stuck here in this painting forever."

"I wish we could too," Jack began, "but I've seen you and Matthew together and he must know you will try to come and help him. He would do it for you. What makes you ever think he would doubt you would do the same for him?"

Jack saw Riley's smile in the fading light of dusk. "Thanks," she said. "I know it's my fault we are in this danger, but I would be lying if I said I wasn't glad you were here."

"You shouldn't be sorry," Jack replied. "I'm not sorry in the least. Even though we are in danger, and in a few hours we are going to have to actually try to rescue your grandfather from a band of real pirates, this is the coolest thing that has ever happened in my whole life."

"I still remember how surprising and exciting it was when I jumped with Matthew for the first time," Riley said.

"What was it like?" Jack asked.

Knowing they had a while to wait, Riley settled back against a palm tree and began to tell Jack the story of her first jump. A little more than two years ago, shortly after Riley's tenth birthday,

Matthew attempted to explain the legacy of art jumping that was woven into their history and had been passed down in his family for generations.

While every member of the family could jump, some had chosen not to do it and preferred a simpler life. Matthew's own father was one of these family members. It was Matthew's grandfather who had told him about the art jumping legacy after his own father had died. His grandfather had been too old to jump with Matthew but had talked him through the process and Matthew ended up making the first of his jumps alone. He had not wanted that to be how it was for Riley and so he sat her down, explained the legacy, and went with her for her first jump.

She knew she should have been shocked at what Matthew had told her about her abilities and the family history. How could you not be when someone tells you that you can jump into a painting? But there was another part of her that simply accepted it. Perhaps it was because it was in her family's blood, but the truth was the idea of it had excited Riley more than it confused or alarmed her.

After Matthew had explained the legacy to Riley he allowed

her to pick the painting. She chose a small painting of a city street fair. She had remembered always liking the painting when it was hung on the walls in the museum and had recently spent a lot of time looking at it while Matthew was repairing some flaking paint. Once the portal had opened into the painting, Matthew and Riley spent hours exploring the various booths at the fair. They played old time games like throwing rings around a stick and trying to knock down pins with a ball. Riley could still remember the smells of all the food being sold in the stalls and could taste the roasted nuts and the homemade chocolate fudge.

What Riley had liked best was watching the other people. She and Matthew had to be careful to blend in as much as possible, but because the scene was in the present day they were able to walk around without standing out and so Riley was able to enjoy watching the other people, imagining what their lives were like, and making up stories about each of them.

"The first few times I jumped with Matthew it was overwhelming. But once you start to let go of how this could possibly be real it's amazing. You are in one place and then you are in a whole other world." There was a smile on Riley's face as she spoke. Clearly jumping had become something she liked to do.

"How often do you jump?" Jack asked.

"Not as much as I'd like," Riley answered. "Matthew goes more. He often jumps without me."

"What do you normally do once you jump?" Jack asked. A million questions were running through his mind and he realized he wanted to know everything about the process.

Riley could see that Jack was interested. It was how she was after Matthew had started to explain it and taken her on her first jump. "It depends what type of painting we jump into, but the main thing we do is just explore. There are rules we try to follow. We try to blend whenever possible. You should always try to stay away from people you find in the world. Being as invisible as possible is key to a successful jump. That lets you look around, see new things, and jump back out again without anyone really noticing you don't belong. For some jumps it's more difficult than others. I remember once I wandered off from Matthew while on a jump and he thought I was lost. He was wild when he found me and made me promise never to jump without him."

Even now Riley remembered the look on Matthew's face

when he said that art jumping was equal parts gift and curse.
She hadn't understood it at that moment but now it was becoming clear. If they didn't have this power they wouldn't be in this danger. Riley refused to think of what would happen if they were trapped here forever. It would be awful enough for her and Matthew, but they would at least be together. She had managed to get Jack involved in this mess. His mother would never know what happened to him. Would everyone wonder what happened? Would there be a police search for the missing trio?

Deep down Riley also wondered if this strange family gift was part of what made her feel so odd and different. She never fit in. What she wasn't sure of was whether her ability to art jump made her that way, or if it was because of her gift that she kept more to herself. All that changed with Jack and now he was involved in this too. She still couldn't figure out how he was able to come along, and she didn't want to think about what Matthew would say when she and Jack came to rescue him. She wondered how mad he would be and how much trouble she had unintentionally made for Jack now that he knew about their art jumping world.

After she had finished, Jack looked at Riley and said, "I know this sounds silly to say right now, but thank you."

"For what?" Riley asked.

"For letting me be a part of this world," Jack began. "I know I wasn't meant to be here. I mean this isn't my family's history but because of you I know about this world and get to be a part of it. I have a feeling Matthew might be mad that I followed you and that I know about all this. I don't know what will happen later, so I just want to say thank you now."

"You're welcome, Jack. And thanks for being here with me," Riley said, smiling. "I don't know if I could have done what we are about to do without your help, and I am glad I don't have to find out."

# Chapter Twelve

Almost two hours had passed as Jack and Riley sat talking about jumping. It was clearly evening now. The sky had cooperated and had given them a full moon and a blanket of stars to help them see better during their rescue attempt.

Realizing the time to move was now, Jack and Riley began their journey through the brush back to the shoreline. Once there they peered down at the beach to observe the scene. It was as they had hoped. A meal had taken place and most of the pirates were sleeping by the fires.

One pirate, who must have been ordered to keep guard, was sitting up on the rocks a good distance from the camp. He would sometimes look towards the others on the beach. Mostly however, he kept his attention on the water and the distant shoreline along the other side of the beach believing these vantage points offered the greatest threat of a possible sneak attack.

Turning their attention next to Matthew, they could see that he was still in the same position with hands and feet tied and the rope gag in his mouth. Even now they could see him struggling to loosen the rope that was tied around his hands.

"We should move now," Riley whispered to Jack. "If we go slowly along the far side of the beach we can reach Matthew by sneaking up to him from behind the side of the rocks."

"I hope he's been able to loosen the ropes a bit. We're going to need him to be untied if we are going to run away quick enough before anyone wakes up," Jack began. Pulling a rock out of his backpack he added, "I found this when we were in the cave. The one side is a bit sharp. Maybe we can use it if we need to help loosen the ropes."

As they talked through the plan, they decided that once they reached the rocks Riley would go to Matthew while Jack stood guard to make sure they weren't spotted. Once they managed to get Matthew free they would need to run quickly as far from the pirate camp as possible.

Neither one of them was completely ready for what needed to

happen next. They knew they had only one chance and so, after giving each other a brief nod, Jack and Riley began their sneak assault across the shoreline.

Moving quickly and quietly, they used the moon's light to guide them and to help keep watch on the guard. As they were moving Jack's stomach growled, making a low gurgling sound. "Sorry, but I think eating nothing since those carrot sticks has finally hit me," Jack whispered.

"I know," Riley said nodding in agreement, "I'm starving. It seems like a waste to not grab some of the leftover food at the fires. What do you think?"

"It's risky," Jack replied, "but I like the way you think. Who's the rebel now?"

"Come on," Riley said, smiling. On their way to the rocks, as they crept past one of the smoldering fires, Jack reached out and grabbed a few of the leftover pieces of fish from the cooking pan. They were still warm as he stuffed them in his backpack. If everything went according to plan they could eat the fish with Matthew after they were safely away from the pirates.

Just as they were moving away from the fire one of the men

dozing gave a half-snore, half-snort. Riley and Jack froze. Afraid to move, they slowly turned and saw that the man had rolled over and fallen back to sleep. Letting out the breath they hadn't realized they had been holding, they continued to move towards the rocks where Matthew was tied up.

Running on the sand was harder than they had expected. When they finally reached the back of the rocks Riley whispered to Jack, "Keep watch and if you see anything whistle low and quick in three sharp notes. I'll meet you and we will retreat back." Jack nodded in agreement as he turned to face out at the pirates.

Matthew, who had been struggling on and off for hours to loosen the ropes around his wrists, had just taken a moment to catch his breath before trying again. More than once since his capture he had forced away the thought that he was forever stuck on this island, having missed the portal to get back home.

He hadn't often jumped into the same painting more than once, but he'd found the island so exciting the first time that he had wanted to go back just one more time to explore. He had gone swimming again in the waterfall's pool and was drying out in the warmth of the entrance of the cave when the pirates had found him. If he had known there was anyone even close to the island he wouldn't have come back. He certainly never thought that the cave was a hiding place for the stolen goods of a pirate crew.

The men had been surprised to find Matthew there. Not knowing how he could have gotten onto their hidden island, they wrongly believed that he was there to steal their treasure. When Matthew tried to explain that he wasn't interested in anything in the cave, one of the men punched him in the face with a strong left hook. Matthew fell hard, causing his glasses to fall off and him to hit his forehead on the rough cave floor. The men tied his wrists together and pulled him through the jungle by a long rope.

Once they reached the camp the pirates had thrown him against the rocks. They tied his feet and gagged him so he would be less of a threat. They must have been waiting to make sure that he was alone. Now it had been a day since they found him and no other people appeared on the island, so the pirates were less concerned about him and had just left him tied up against the rocks. Twice one of the men had given him a bit of water and a scrap of food, but nothing else.

It had become clear to Matthew that he wasn't going to be set free. At one point he overheard two pirates talking together behind the rocks. The pirates would be leaving in the morning and the captain was trying to decide whether to leave him tied up to starve on the island or bring him with them on board the ship. Once they were far enough out in the middle of the ocean he would be dropped overboard and left to drown.

Neither option was acceptable to Matthew so he had been furiously struggling to break free from the ropes ever since. In the back of his mind he knew that there was a chance that Riley would come looking for him. As much as he wanted to get home and get back to her, he worried about her jumping into the painting and getting into trouble. If there was even the slightest chance that she would come back to try to get him, he needed to be free and away from these pirates so she didn't end up captured as well. He also knew if she didn't come, and he was in fact stuck here on this island, that he needed to be free from the pirates before they finished him off for good.

Matthew worried about what would happen to Riley if he didn't make it back. He feared that she would never know what happened to him.

Pushing those thoughts from his head and focusing on the task at hand, he was about to start trying to again loosen the ropes around his wrists when he heard a slight rustling sound behind the rocks.

Struggling to turn toward the noise, he was afraid he must be dreaming when he saw Riley creeping towards him, her eyes wide and brimming with tears. "Matthew," she exclaimed in a whisper. "Are you okay? We've come to get you and go home." As she spoke Riley removed the gag from Matthew's mouth.

"Riley," Matthew softly cried. "Thank God you've come, but it is too dangerous. We need to get out of here right away!"

"I know," she replied, "but we have to get you free first so you can move. Let's see how tight these knots are." The knots had loosened thanks to Matthew's efforts and so with just a little extra work Riley was able to untie the rope and set his wrists free.

The pain in his wrists from being bent in that position for so long was great. Ignoring the ache, Matthew immediately began to untie the rope around his ankles.

Seeing him struggle Riley pulled the stone from her pocket

and said, "Here, maybe this will help." Sawing back and forth with the sharp edge of the rock against the rope it only took a minute for it to be loose enough for Matthew to break free.

"Can you stand?" Riley asked.

"I don't know. I've been sitting for so many hours, but I'll manage," Matthew said, trying to put a brave face on although he was greatly worried. He struggled to stand. First he managed to get to his knees. Using the rock face and Riley's shoulder for support, he was then able to stand. His legs felt as loose as cooked spaghetti noodles, but the longer he stood the less the ground seemed to be moving beneath him.

"We need to move quietly," Riley whispered.

"There's a guard watching over at the rocks to the left," Matthew warned.

"We know," Riley replied. "We won't make a move until we know he's looking in the other direction. We also need to be careful not to wake any of the other sleeping men."

"Who is 'we'?" Matthew asked. But his confusion quickly turned to a surprise that bordered on disbelief when, sneaking past the rocks, he saw Jack crouched down keeping a lookout over the entire camp. "Jack, what are you doing here? I mean *how* are you here?"

"Matthew," Jack quietly exclaimed, rushing over to give him a hug. "I'm so glad to see you. We need to move fast and get as far away from here as we can."

The need to move quickly prevented Matthew from fully processing all that was happening. He followed Riley as she took the lead away from the rocks. Still unsteady, Matthew leaned on Jack a bit as he struggled to keep up. Matthew's weakness forced them to move slowly, but they were making ground getting away from the camp when Matthew stumbled on a piece of driftwood.

Lurching forward, he made a small cry as his knees buckled. Jack and Riley moved quickly to steady him and help him stand.

The cry had drawn the attention of the guard, who looking in the direction of the sound, could just barely make out the forms of the three figures on the beach. The pirate jumped up in the hopes of getting a better look. It was then that he saw Matthew running across the beach aided by two other figures.

He began to yell, "Escape, escape!" at the top of his voice. To further the alarm he picked up a conch shell and blew into it as loudly as he could. The resounding noise was a deep, vibrating tone that seemed to fill the entire island shore.

"Run!" Riley yelled at the top of her voice and they all began to run.

Fortunately, the food and drink that the pirates had enjoyed for the large part of the evening had made their response slow. It took some time for them to fully wake and realize what was happening.

"The old man's escaped," yelled one of the pirates after seeing the cut and discarded ropes that had once tied the prisoner's hands and feet. Slowly all the pirates became alert and aware of what was going on.

"There, over there!" another shouted. "Don't let them get away."

As if on cue some of the pirates began to chase after Matthew, Riley, and Jack. Having a bit of distance on them, the three were able to make it inside the brush before the pirates could see exactly what direction they went.

# Chapter Thirteen

Inside the jungle Matthew, Jack, and Riley began a mad dash through the brush. What had been a difficult trek in daylight would have been almost impossible in the dark but the full moon gave just enough light to allow the three to see a few steps in front of them as they continued to push forward.

The pirates didn't know exactly where they had gone but did see them go into the jungle. Matthew, Riley, and Jack could hear the noise of them following not far behind.

They ran on for a while until Riley reached her hand back to stop them. "Wait," she whispered, trying to catch her breath as they came to a stop. "Do you hear that?"

"It's the waterfall," Jack said in reply. "They're sure to search inside the cave but maybe we can hide nearby without being discovered."

## About The Author

Jessica DiPalma is an art historian and writer.
She lives in New York.